Peabody Publ
Columbia City

P9-CAO-810

J 3-4 PAPER CLARKE
Clarke, Jane,
Sherman swaps shells /
[written by] Jane Clarke ;
[illustrated by] Ant Parker.
DEC 23 '04

DISCARD

For everyone at Antwerp International School – JC

For Dizzie and Enid – AP

Crabtree Publishing Company

www.crabtreebooks.com

PMB 16A, 350 Fifth Avenue,
Suite 3308,
New York, NY
10118

612 Welland Avenue,
St. Catharines,
Ontario, Canada
L2M 5V6

Published by Crabtree Publishing Company in 2004
Published in 2001 by Random House Children's Books and Red Fox

Cataloging-in-Publication data

Clark, Jane.
Sherman swaps shells/ written by Jane Clark ; illustrated by Ant Parker.
p. cm. – (Flying foxes)
Summary: Sherman the hermit crab finds that shopping for new
shells isn't easy, especially when his mother thinks he should chose the
sensible outerwear and he just wants to appear cool.
ISBN 0-7787-1485-3 (RLB) – ISBN 0-7787-1531-0 (PB)
[1. Nature–Fiction. 2. Environment–Fiction.] I. Parker, Ant ill. II.
Title. III. Series.

2003022720
LC

Text copyright © Jane Clarke 2001
Illustrations copyright © Ant Parker 2001

The rights of Jane Clarke and Ant Parker to be identified as the author
and illustrator of this work have been asserted by them in accordance with
the Copyright, Designs and Patents Act, 1988.

Set in Cheltenham Book Infant

1 2 3 4 5 6 7 8 9 0 Printed and bound in Malaysia by Tien Wah Press 0 9 8 7 6 5 4 3

All rights reserved. No part of this publication may be reproduced, stored in a retrieval
system, or transmitted in any form or by any means, electronic, mechanical, photocopying,
recording or otherwise, without the prior permission of the publishers.

Sherman Swaps Shells

Jane Clarke
Ant Parker

DISCARD

Peabody Public Library
Columbia City, IN

"Sherman," said his mom, "you need a new shell."

"But I like this one," Sherman said.

"Look at the state of it! You've chipped it playing clawball. It won't keep you safe any more."

"I'll be careful," Sherman said.

Peabody Public Library
Columbia City, IN

"It's covered in tar and it's much too small," his mom said. "Your shell doesn't fit you any more. You've grown out of it."

"There's plenty of room at the end!" Sherman wriggled his tail. It scraped against the pebble collection he kept at the bottom of his shell.

I hate swapping.

"You can't wear the same shell forever," said his mom. "It's time for you to swap shells." Sherman's mom took him by the claw. They scuttled to the shell heap.

"There's a lot to choose from," said
his mom.
"The waves bring in new shells all the time.
This looks like a good one. Try it on."

"Someone might see," Sherman said.

"There's no need to be shy," his mom said.

Sherman tried it on. "It's too tight," he said.

"Yes," agreed his mom. "How about that
green one over there?"

Sherman slipped out of his old
shell and into the green one.
"It's very nice," said his mom.
"It's very heavy," said Sherman.
"It's just right," said his mom.

Oh, Sherman, you do look nice!

I want one like that!

A teenager strolled past. He was wearing a shell with huge spikes.

"Wow!" said Sherman. "Can I have one of those? Please?"

"Those shells are hard to find in your size," his mom said.

11

"Here's one," said Sherman. "I'll try it on."
"It's far too big," said his mom.

It doesn't fit.

"Everyone's wearing them like this,"
said Sherman.

"Take it off," said his mom. "You can have
one when you're older."

"It's not fair," said Sherman.

"How about this one?" his mom said.
"It's just like your old shell. Put it on."

"Do I have to?"

"Yes," said his mom. "If you're good,
I'll take you to Urchin Express."

Sherman dived out of his old shell into
the new one.

"Get out of my shell!" roared a voice.
Sherman shot out backward.

"Didn't your mother teach you to knock?"
the old hermit crab grumbled.

"Sherman!" his mom was lobster pink.
"I'm very sorry," she told the old crab.
"He needs a new shell, you see. Come
along, Sherman. We'll look over there."

Sherman scuttled to the top of the shell heap.

I'm stuck!

"I like this one," he said,
pointing to a spiky shell.
"It will never fit," his mom said.
"It will, look." Sherman squeezed into
the shell. "It's a bit tight," he said.

"Take it off then," said his mom.

"Mom!" Sherman tried to wriggle out of the shell. "I'm stuck . . ."

"I knew it," said his mom. "Our bodies curve to the right. Most shells have spirals that curve to the right. This one curves to the left. That's why you're stuck."

"I'll pull you out," his mom said. She grabbed Sherman's legs with her powerful claws and heaved.

"Oooooof!"

Sherman popped out. He counted his legs. They were all still there. He slunk back into his old shell.

"Now Sherman," his mom said. "We can spend all day trying to find another shell. Or we can go back and get the green one that was just right, and go to Urchin Express."

"What's the tide?" asked Sherman.

"High tide. There will be plenty of fresh plankton."

"Okay," said Sherman, "we'll get the green shell."

Sherman swapped shells. He emptied his pebble collection into the bottom of the new shell. There was plenty of room inside.

He could collect more now.

"What am I going to do with my old shell?" asked Sherman.

"Leave it here," said his Mom. "Someone else might want it."

Sherman patted the shell with his claw. "Goodbye, Old Shell," he said. "I'll miss you."

It was fun playing clawball with you.

Urchin Express was very busy. It was full of young anemones waving their tentacles. There was a long line. They crawled toward the counter.

Why are those limpets pushing?

They ordered, and
found an empty rock
and sat down.

"How's the plankton
shake?" asked his mom.
"Delicious." Sherman
slurped the last drops
through the straw.

"Disgusting," said his mom.
"It isn't even dead yet."
   She nibbled on
her piece of
rotten fish.

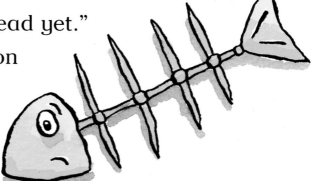

"My new shell is heavy," Sherman said.
"It's a good solid shell," said his mom. "Very sensible."
"It would look great with anemones stuck on it," said Sherman.

Anemones are cool!

30

"You're not sticking anemones on a brand new shell!" said his mom.

"But anemones are cool!" said Sherman. "And they're great for playing tide-and-seek. No one would find me if I had anemones on my shell. Why can't I have anemones? It's not fair! I wish I had my old shell back!"

"Cheer up!" his mom said. "Worse things happen at sea."

Anemones are silly!

Suddenly a shadow blotted out
the sun. Urchin Express went dark.
The shadow reached into the
tide pool.

I'm off!

Hide!

Peabody Public Library
Columbia City, IN

The shadow scooped up Sherman!
Higher and higher he went. Higher than
high tide.

Sherman was frightened. He hid inside his
new shell. The shadow's giant claw turned
him upside down.

"This is a nice shell," the shadow said.
"I think I'll keep it."

It nipped me!

"I'm not a shell! I'm a hermit crab!"
Sherman nipped the shadow as hard as he
could. The shadow yelled,

"Ow, ow, ow!"

Sherman **flew** through the air.

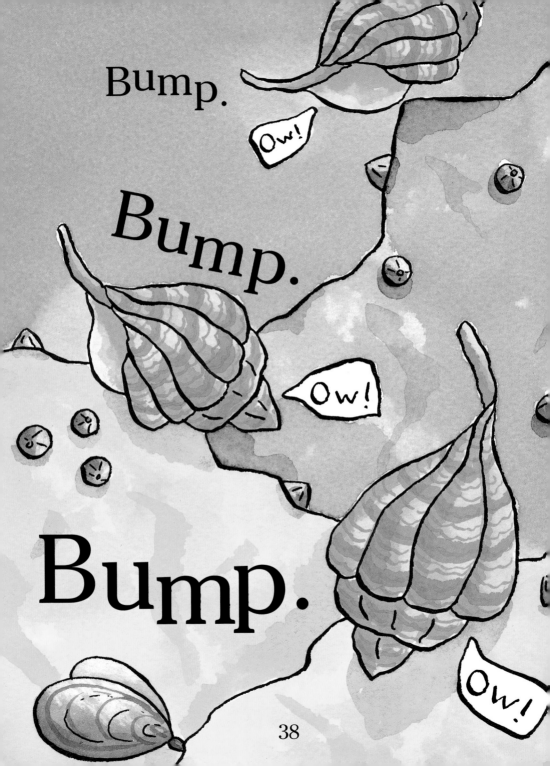

Sherman bounced down the rocks and fell into the pool.

Sunlight danced across the tide pool. The shadow was gone.

Plop.

"Sherman! Are you okay?"

"I . . . I think so."

"It's a good job you were wearing your new shell," said his mom. "Your old one would have broken!"

41

"What was that shadow?" Sherman asked.

"It was a Person," his mom said. "You have to hide from People."

"People wouldn't see me if I had anemones on my shell."

"Hmmm," said his mom.

I might get some too!

"So can I stick anemones on my shell?"

"Okay," said his mom.

"Great!" said Sherman. "I think I'll like my new shell."

et your anemones here.

No one will find me now!

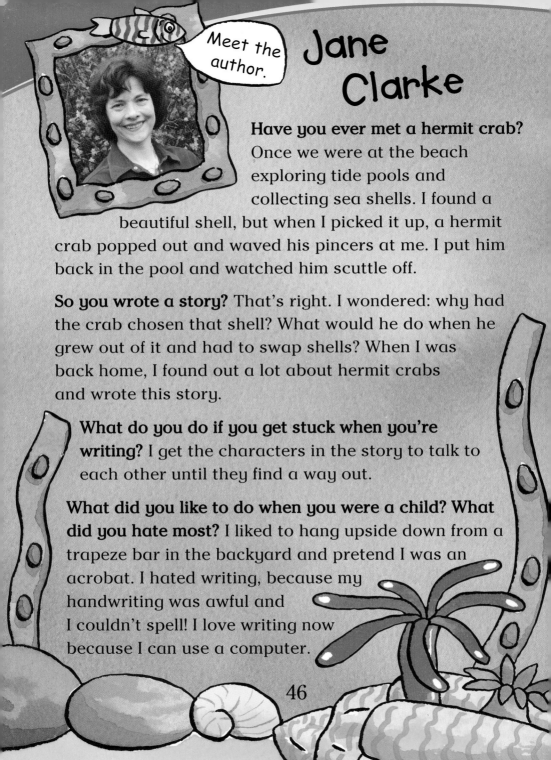

Meet the author.

Jane Clarke

Have you ever met a hermit crab? Once we were at the beach exploring tide pools and collecting sea shells. I found a beautiful shell, but when I picked it up, a hermit crab popped out and waved his pincers at me. I put him back in the pool and watched him scuttle off.

So you wrote a story? That's right. I wondered: why had the crab chosen that shell? What would he do when he grew out of it and had to swap shells? When I was back home, I found out a lot about hermit crabs and wrote this story.

What do you do if you get stuck when you're writing? I get the characters in the story to talk to each other until they find a way out.

What did you like to do when you were a child? What did you hate most? I liked to hang upside down from a trapeze bar in the backyard and pretend I was an acrobat. I hated writing, because my handwriting was awful and I couldn't spell! I love writing now because I can use a computer.

46

Ant Parker

Meet the illustrator.

Have you ever met a hermit crab? I grew up a long way from the sea, but we went on school field trips to visit the coast. We would collect things and bring them back – not living things of course! I don't think I ever saw a hermit crab, but we found shrimp, starfish, and jellyfish.

How long did it take to paint the pictures in this book? Shells are difficult to draw so I had to do a lot of research. I found some very good sites about hermit crabs on the Internet. Then I drew the pictures in pencil. Next, I painted them with ink and watercolor. This last part took about a month.

Where do you live? I live in London, England but I go to the coast a lot. In summer, I go swimming. In winter, I go on long walks with my dog Bramble. She likes to roll in the seaweed left by high tide. Often she comes home with old crab shells stuck in her coat!

Did you always like to draw? I have liked to draw since I was very young.

Will you try and write or draw a story?

Let your ideas take flight with

Flying Foxes

Digging for Dinosaurs
by Judy Waite and Garry Parsons

Only Tadpoles Have Tails
by Jane Clarke and Jane Gray

The Magic Backpack
by Julia Jarman and Adriano Gon

Slow Magic
by Pippa Goodhart and John Kelly

Sherman Swaps Shells
by Jane Clarke and Ant Parker

That's Not Right!
by Alan Durant and Katharine McEwen

DISCARD

Peabody Public Library
Columbia City, IN